Occ

The bear
and
the people

The bear
and
the people

Written and illustrated by

Reiner Zimnik

Translated from the German by Nina Ignatowicz

HARPER & ROW, PUBLISHERS, New York, Evanston, San Francisco, London

T 4uiea

172 79

The bear
and
the people

Well, there was
a man once

and
he had a bear.

The man wouldn't say where he came from, and no one knew his name. People simply called him "Bearman," and this pleased the man.

The bear didn't have a name, either. The man called him "Brown One," which was fine with the bear.

The Bearman had two friends: the bear and Dear God.

He had an iron frying pan, a horn which could play only one note, and seven balls.

He had no buried treasure in the woods, he could not perform magic, and he did not believe in magic spirits. There were only three unusual things about him—he could understand the language of bears, he was kind, and he could juggle seven balls.

The bear was brown and knew how to dance. Whenever the man played a tune on his barrel organ, the bear would stand on his hind legs and dance to the music. He had an iron ring through his nose, and a muzzle, like every respectable dancing bear.

But he was never kept on a chain like other dancing bears. And he never wanted to run away from his Bearman. Why would he? He danced, and for this he was fed. On Sundays he got an extra pound of honey. And that was all he knew.

When he danced his little eyes sparkled, and sometimes he would wink at the Bearman and growl softly:

"Ho, Man, how's my dancing? Very good, hm?" And the man would look pleased and whisper softly:

"Very good, Brown One, and so harmonious!"

They traveled from village to village, and they were a part of the highway like the knotty old apple trees and whitethorn bushes.

And they walked slowly and steadily, taking three steps to each breath.

And the farmers in the fields would watch for them. Sharpening their scythes and wiping the sweat from their brows, the farmers would squint their eyes and peer down the highway.

Whenever they saw the two in the distance they would call to each other: "The bear, the bear!" On such days they stopped their work early.

The children rejoiced in the village. "The bear is here! The bear is here!" and they made a circle around the two and jumped all around them. They pulled the bear's fur and ears, and climbed on his shaggy back. And the very little ones stood on the garden gates, whispering excitedly: "The beh, the beh!"

"Ha, ha!" said the man to the bear. "Happy children, eh, Brown One?"

And the bear growled: "Hmhmhmhm" and grunted with joy.

The children called out: "Show us a trick! Show us a trick!"

They hung on the arms of the Bearman and begged him till he finally showed them a trick. He took a ball out of his pocket, placed it on the back of his hand and then let it roll slowly over his arm, shoulders, back, and down to the tip of his left foot. Then he sent it high up into the air and caught it again with his right hand.

Then the Bearman went to the town bulletin board and wrote with white chalk:

I and the bear will perform great ## tricks this evening in front of the church and everyone is invited cordially

People would have known without the bulletin board, but since it was the custom, and since the Bearman knew how to write, he always wrote with chalk on bulletin boards.

In the evening everyone, except those who were sick and had to stay in bed, was in front of the church.

The Bearman banged his pan seven times with a wooden hammer. It sounded like a gong. Then he cried out loudly and clearly: "My dear ladies and gentlemen, the performance begins!" And then he said softly to the bear: "You know, I go on first."

He took two small red balls out of his pocket and began to juggle them. Every now and then a farmhand would cry out: "Some trick! I can do it too! I'm sure I can do it too!" But then the Bearman took a green ball out of his pocket and juggled three balls. As the three balls whirled through the air, the Bearman quickly reached into his trouser pocket, and the children cried out excitedly: "Four balls, four balls!" Soon they were all shouting: "Five balls, five balls!" And then even the farmhands who were not impressed before gasped in amazement: "Look, six balls, six balls!" When the Bearman reached into his pocket for the last time and spun the seventh ball into the air, the audience went wild. "Seven balls, seven balls!" they shouted. "Has anyone ever seen a man who could juggle seven balls? This is fantastic, fantastic! Nobody else can do it!" And everyone clapped and whistled and praised the Bearman. The Bearman made one ball after another disappear into his trouser pocket, bowed, and said: "Thank you."

Then he banged his gong again and cried out:

"The-e-e dancing bear-r-r-r!"

He said to the bear: "Now it's your turn!"

He picked up his barrel organ and began to turn the handle. The bear rose on his hind legs. At first he turned slowly and with difficulty, then faster and faster, till finally he was dancing to the music that came from the organ box.

"Look! He's dancing!" whispered the people, as if each one couldn't see for himself. "Look, a dancing bear. And his eyes sparkle." They all gasped and the bear winked at the Bearman and growled softly:

"Ho, Man, how's my dancing today? Good, hm?"

And the Bearman whispered back softly: "Very good, Brown One, and so harmonious!"

When the music stopped, the Bearman and the bear bowed. And while the people were still noisy and excited, the Bearman passed around a china plate. As almost everyone was poor then, they had to dig deep into their coat pockets to find even a copper coin. While this was happening, the children ran home and brought back honey for the bear.

In the morning the Bearman and the bear were back on the highway. The man breathed evenly, taking three steps to each breath, and the bear followed in his bear-trot. Not a word passed between them. The man peered at the horizon where the thin line of the highway disappeared into the distance, and the bear listened to the scratching of his boots. It was always the same. Even in thunder and lightning, when the storm lashed down upon the land and every creature hid in his nook in fright, the two could be seen walking, calm and erect, taking three steps to each breath.

In the evening they sat near a spring, and the man lit a fire and prepared food. When both were full, the bear scratched at the man's leg and growled: "The story, Bearman!"

Though there is an infinite number of stars, the man could tell a story about every star. And the bear would pester the Bearman and not let him go to sleep until he had told him a story.

The man waited for the embers to die out under the pan. Then he braced his hands around his knees and told the story of the black bear who each night pulls a wagon of four sparkling stars through the sky.

And the bear sat as still as a mouse and pricked up his ears.

Then the Bearman spoke to Dear God: "Dear God, now I will play a couple of notes on my horn for You and the bear." He always said "a couple of notes," even though he could play only one single note. But he played it so softly and so beautifully that all the animals in the forest raised their heads and listened. The bear laid his head down on his front paws and growled softly. And Dear God must have liked the humble music, because the woods stopped rustling every time the Bearman played his horn. As the note died away, its echo played a tiny melody. And it was as pure and clear as silver jewels.

"Listen!" whispered the man into the bear's ear. "Can you hear it?"

The bear nodded, and neither made a sound.

Then they lay down and slept. The man warmed himself against the bear's fur and the night covered them in a thick, black mantle.

Days passed and the two traveled through many villages. The man juggled seven balls and the bear danced. And each evening at twilight the man played a note on his horn for the bear, and for Dear God who was his friend.

Wherever they went, the people rejoiced.

Only the dogs growled angrily. They tore at their chains when the bear trotted past them. The dogs of the whole land were jealous of the bear who could dance, but they did not dare to attack him. They feared his mighty paws.

One day the Bearman and the bear met the Henman, and they were very happy. They hadn't seen the Henman for many years.

The three sat around the fire—the Bearman, the Henman, and the bear. When they were full, the Bearman told them a new story about stars, and then all three listened to the tiny melody. "Do you hear it?" whispered the Bearman. "It comes every night, after I play my horn." The Henman closed his eyes and cupped his hands to his ears.

18

"Yes," he whispered, "yes, yes, yes, I can hear it too." And he beamed with pleasure.

But when they settled down for the night the Henman began to moan. The Bearman said to him: "I see you are sad and troubled, brother." The Henman replied: "The Dudas have come, and they steal chickens wherever they go. I am an old man; what will I do when they steal my chickens?"

But the Bearman said: "Have no fear, Henman. I am strong, and when there is a bear around nobody will steal any chickens!" The Henman was happy and was no longer afraid.

The next morning they saw the Dudas on the highway—the old Duda, who could balance on a rolling ball, and his two sons. The elder son could juggle six balls. They had three wives, an armful of children, and a monkey who could beat the drum. Their wagon was painted red and white. They also had a camel.

"Why do they need a camel?" the Bearman asked the Henman.

The Henman said: "They let people ride on his back. One ride, four coins." The Bearman grumbled: "Swindlers!" and complained to the bear and Dear God that the old Duda charged four coins for one single ride.

At this time each year there was a big Fair. Wagon after wagon filed along the highway. They came from near and far, all heading for the town. The farmers brought smoked ham and butter and cheese; horsedealers came with

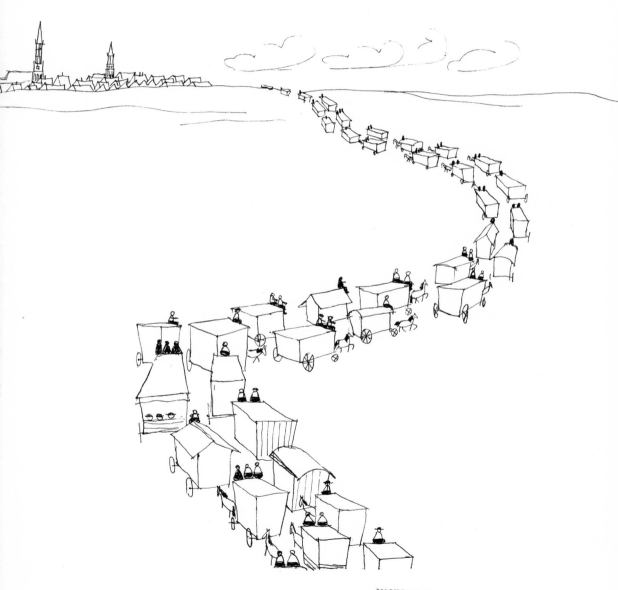

their steeds and shepherds with carts full of wool. There were pigeon-handlers, silversmiths, ragmen, and entertainers. And the Dudas and the Henman and the Bearman and the bear followed in the long procession.

There was rattling and clattering, neighing and bleating, and whips cracking. "Whoa!" shouted the drivers and "Move on!" The axles groaned, the women quarreled. And on top of all this, the sun scorched and the yellow dust lay finger-thick on the spokes of the wheels, on the horses, and on the faces of the travelers.

"Ho, you've never seen so many wagons, eh Brown One?" the man asked the bear, when they were finally rumbling through the narrow streets of the town. The bear shook the dust off his fur and growled: "Mm, never!"

The marketplace was filled with tents—yellow, gray, and blue-and-white striped. There were shooting booths, drinking booths, and booths where one could see a mermaid for a coin. Then came the tents of the fire-swallowers and tightrope walkers. There were conjurers who could pull two white doves out of one high hat, others who could swallow an egg and then shake it out of the sleeve, and still others who could pierce a basket with ten sabers and then out would step a young lady, lively and unharmed. And there were the Dudas. They gave rides on the camel for four coins a ride; the old Duda balanced on his rolling sphere; the older son juggled six balls; the women read people's fortunes; and the monkey beat the drum.

But there was only one dancing bear, and there was only one man who could juggle seven balls and that was the Bearman.

The two were surrounded by people in no time. "Seven balls, seven balls!" they all shouted. "Look, a dancing bear! Can you imagine? A dancing bear!"

As the Henman made his way through the swelling crowd with a white plate collecting coins for his two friends, the crowd began to leave the red-and-white striped tent where the monkey beat the drum and where the Duda women jingled their bells. More and more people hurried over to the dancing bear.

The old Duda cursed everything under the sun and sent his elder son to challenge the Bearman. The crowd was still shouting: "Look, seven balls, seven balls! Nobody else can do that. Only the Bearman can do that!" The young Duda forced his way through the crowd and burst out laughing: "Hahaha! Big deal! I can do that too. I can juggle seven balls without turning a hair!"

"You lie!" roared the Bearman. "If you want us to believe that, step forward and show us your art!"

"That's right!" shouted the people. "You better show us! We want to see it!" The Duda's son stood up on a box and shouted: "Okay, you people. Come with me to the red-and-white striped tent. There I will stand alongside the Bearman and juggle seven balls!"

"Go!" shouted the people. "Go over there, Bearman!" they cried. "We want to see if he is telling the truth!"

"Did you hear that?" the Bearman asked Dear God. "Did you hear that, bear? Did you hear that, Henman?" he asked. "A cunning scoundrel, this Duda," he snarled. And as the crowd shoved and hooted and the farmhands called him a coward, the Bearman took his seven balls and went over to the tent of the Dudas. The two men stood very close to each other with their legs apart, and made sure once more that the balls lay loosely in their pockets. The old Duda, rubbing his hands together, laughed maliciously. He had never had such a large crowd around his tent.

"Let's go, you two!" shouted a butcher. "Get moving!"

Two balls whirled through the air, and the people said: "Two balls, two balls!" Then there were three, four. "Five balls," cried the people. "Six balls, yes, six balls!" Then quickly both men reached into their trouser pockets for the seventh time and everyone cried out in praise: "Seven balls! He told the truth! Seven balls! Bravo, bravo! Seven balls!"

But the Bearman was white with rage. He whispered: "Dear God, help me!" With the speed of lightning the young Duda had tossed the seventh ball from his pocket over to the Bearman, so that the Duda was juggling only six balls while the Bearman juggled eight. And no one but Dear God and the Bearman and the Duda knew about it. "He played a dirty trick on me, the scoundrel," the Bearman whispered to Dear God. "Soon he will throw me another ball, and then I am lost."

With the balls whirling in the air, the Bearman carefully took four steps to the side. Then he turned to the crowd and shouted: "Hey, you people, count the balls. Count them one by one!"

When the people had finished counting and discovered the fraud, they became angry and excited. "Cheat!" they shouted, pointing at the Duda's son. "Scoundrel, rogue, liar! We want our money back!" they shouted. "Swindler, thief, rascal!" they shouted and surged toward the tent. And if the young Duda hadn't managed to flee quickly through the back door, they would have beaten him up.

The Bearman put the balls back into his pocket, spat on the ground, and walked away, proud as a king, calm and erect, taking three steps to each breath. And the people followed him with respect.

The old Duda raved as it became empty around his tent once again. His women hid themselves in their red-and-white striped wagon, and the monkey, who had no part in this deceit, climbed up on the roof and beat the drum slowly and regularly, just as before. The Bearman told his bear and the Henman about the Duda's fraud and how Dear God had helped him. And the people once again gathered around the dancing bear and filled the plate with coppers and nickels.

Suddenly there was a commotion in the crowd. People began to whisper to each other, and then they all ran back to the old Duda's tent. No one remained to watch the dancing bear.

The Duda women, wearing only their red skirts, were dancing in front of the red-and-white striped tent. The people ogled and gaped; they almost broke their necks trying to take in everything that was going on. The old Duda cracked out the rhythm with a dog-whip, and his sons mingled with the people and picked their pockets. And business was good.

28

A little way off stood the Bearman juggling his seven balls. But besides Dear God his audience consisted of the bear, the Henman, and two cats. And that's not much for a man who can juggle seven balls.

The bear trotted up to him and growled: "The horn, Man, the horn!"

And then, amid the clatter and constant jingling of the naked women, the people heard the gentle note. It was so beautiful that they were all spell-bound and listened to the note. And then the tiny melody filled the air. And

it was as pure and clear as silver jewels. The dancing women turned their backs in shame. The old Duda cursed and raged, and the monkey beat the drum. The people left the red-and-white striped tent and made a circle around the man and the bear. And there they stayed for the rest of the day.

As the pale moon rose from behind the wagons, all the performers counted their money. The call of the screech owl echoed through the tents, and the cats sneaked by the wheels and shafts, and the performers went to sleep. The Henman's ram pricked up his ears, snorted, and scraped with his right front hoof. This woke the Henman. The Henman pulled at the Bearman's sleeve and whispered: "Bearman, my ram has scraped with his right front hoof. Hey, Bearman," he said and trembled, "do you think someone wants to steal my chickens?"

"Have no fear," said the Bearman, "where there is a bear, no chickens will be stolen, believe me."

But the bear also growled and pricked up his ears. The three decided to keep watch. The screech owl called eighteen times and then they saw three men coming toward them from across the field.

When the creeping figures were quite near, the Bearman recognized the old Duda and his two sons. "It is the old Duda with his two sons," he whispered to his friends, "and I'll be damned if the old rogue doesn't mean to do us harm." The Bearman noticed that the old Duda was holding the leather dog-whip in his hand. One of the sons carried a club, and the other a bared saber. "But they didn't bring along a sack," he thought. "One always brings a sack when going chicken stealing."

The Bearman whispered: "Dear God, there will be a wild rumpus. Help us."

The old Duda swore through his teeth when he saw that the Bearman and his friends were awake. He stopped four steps away from them, rolled his eyes and said with hatred: "Hand over the horn!"

The bear pricked up his ears and spat.

"The Horn!" repeated the old Duda in a cutting voice. "If you value your life," added one of the sons, and raised his club. The third Duda cut the air with his saber and mocked: "Or perhaps you think we are afraid of a giddy bear, huh?"

The Bearman didn't say a word, but he didn't take his eyes off the old Duda.

"I'm counting to three!" shouted the old Duda.

"One!" The bear crouched down low.

"Two!" The Bearman reached for the iron pan.

"Three! Go to hell!" thundered the old Duda.

The whip whizzed through the air and caught the bear at his most sensitive spot—where the ring pierces his nose. The bear howled and twisted with pain. But before the old Duda could inflict another blow, the bear leaped at him

and tore at his skin and clothes. The second Duda, swinging his club, sprang to the old Duda's aid. But the Bearman crashed the pan down on his arm. The Henman grabbed red-hot ashes from the fire with his bare hands and threw them in the face of the third Duda. "Goddammit, I can't see a thing, I can't see a thing!" he cursed and, like a madman, lashed the air around him with his saber. "Come, Satan! Help me!" he yelled. Just then he was knocked down by the bear and had to fight for his life. Frantically the Dudas defended themselves. They punched and kicked with all their strength, like the highway robbers they were. But the Bearman and the bear were stronger. When the second Duda's shoulders were pinned to the ground and the Bearman had his knee on his chest, the old Duda begged for mercy: "I swear by all the stars in heaven that the Dudas will do you no harm as long as I live." The Bearman released them, and calmed the bear.

Torn and battered and not saying a word, the three Dudas dragged themselves away. They hated the man and the bear, but they feared them even more. And that is why the promise was not broken as long as they lived.

The Bearman put healing herbs on his wounds and the wounds of his friends, and the Henman went down to the spring to cool his burned hands. Then they thanked Dear God and lay down to rest. And the screech owl called and the stars twinkled as if nothing had happened.

Now the three walked along the highway—the Bearman, the bear, and the Henman. The days got longer and the nights shorter. And as the moon became full for the fourth time, the farmers cut the wheat. The Henman took leave of his friends and rode off into the fields with his chickens.

Winter came and the farmers and farmhands gathered around the frozen lakes and played the game of curling.

There came the time of clear skies; the apple trees were in bloom and the colorful birds came from Africa.

White dust appeared on the highway, and crickets chirped, and again the farmers cut the wheat.

The first frost came. A hundred thousand little spiders put a spell on the land and the colorful birds flew back to Africa.

And leaves died and bonfires burned. The mornings were cold and the frost and thin ice lay over the puddles, and the storms came, and the snow, and a new winter.

Years passed. The shoots which the farmers planted in their gardens the first time the man and the bear passed their village were full-grown trees now, and bore fruit.

Then came the motorcars. At first there were only a few; their drivers waved their hats when they drove past the Bearman and the bear.

As time passed, more and more cars began to appear on the highway. They kept getting bigger, they smoked and thundered, and they went faster and faster.

Soon there was no more room on the highways for the performers. Now they could travel only by the small roads through the fields.

The old Duda was dead. His elder son, the one who could juggle six balls, learned a trade, built himself a house, and settled down. The other son became a thief, went to jail, and spent the rest of his life on bread and water.

The sun, wind, and rain had chiseled a thousand furrows and folds on the Bearman's face, and his hair had become snow-white. But still the man and the bear could be seen making their way, calm and erect, taking three steps to each breath.

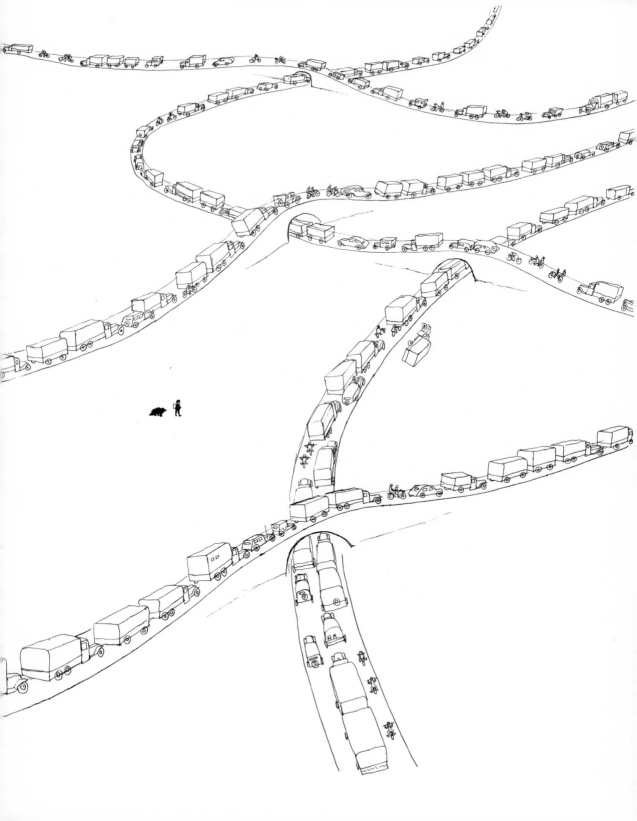

There is a time of year when the land is like a nightmare—the days between the last grim frosts of winter and the time of clear skies. The warm winds descend from the mountains; they whistle and gurgle and tear at the roofs. And the old tree-trunks groan and creak under their scabby barks. Green light flickers on the horizon, and the dirty clouds lash down on the gray snowfields. On such nights the farmers bolt the doors of their houses and barns to stop witches from getting in and making mischief for man and beast. And no man dares to venture out into the village street.

Soaked to the skin, the man and the bear plodded through the snow looking for a dry barn. It was cold, and the watchdogs howled in all the villages.

The bear growled uneasily. Sometimes he stopped in his tracks, listened, looked about him, and hesitated before taking another step.

At one bend in the road, they looked back and saw a small dog following them. At the next bend six dogs were following them. The bear's eyes sparked ominously.

The Bearman hurled a rock at the pack. The curs retreated, but they came back. They followed the two without a sound, step by step.

More and more dogs appeared. They came from farms, woods, and from behind bushes. What a strange procession the Bearman led! Sometimes the whistling of the wind would stop for a second and the man and the bear could hear the panting of the dogs. And they saw their tongues hanging out of their mouths and they saw their bared fangs.

"They are all after us," growled the bear. He turned to the dogs, spread out his hind legs, crouched forward and pricked up his ears. The Bearman knew that a terrible battle would ensue and he told Dear God about it.

The Bearman blew the horn. And as the gentle note mingled with the whistling wind, the dogs froze in their tracks. Only their green eyes, fixed on the Bearman's horn, were aflame. They seemed to want to tear away the horn with their eyes. As long as the Bearman played the horn, the pack didn't move. But little by little the rain seeped into the horn, and the note grew fainter and fainter.

When the horn became silent, the first dog struck. The bear broke the dog's spine with one single blow of his paw. And he did the same to the dogs that followed. The dogs attacked one at a time, not making a sound and gasping faintly as they died. The Bearman was exultant. "AAH!" he shouted, swinging his iron pan.

As though awakened from a magic spell, howling wildly, the whole pack struck at the man and the bear. The man backed up against a tree and smashed his iron pan down on the skull of every dog that tried to get at his throat. The bear sank his teeth into the bodies of his attackers; his paws were red with their blood. When the dogs tried to bite through his fur, the bear rolled himself on the ground and crushed their bodies under his mighty weight. But for every dead dog, three new curs rushed into the battle. And as the strength of the bear and the man slowly diminished, the pack kept growing.

The noise of the uneven battle could be heard far into the country—the howling of the pack, the bellowing of the bear, and the dull crashing sound of the iron pan as the Bearman smashed it down on his attackers.

By the time the farmers arrived on the scene and scattered the pack with their iron sticks and axes, the man and the bear were at the end of their strength. The man leaned panting against the tree, and the bear's flanks were bleeding. But they were alive.

From that day on, people noticed a slight stoop in the Bearman's shoulders, as though he were carrying a heavy load. Also, he stopped more often on his journey and spoke to his friend, Dear God. Or he would nudge the bear, point around them, and say: "Do you see everything, Brown One?

How beautiful it is. How vast and how beautiful!"

"I know," growled the bear. "You have already said it a hundred times."

When the trees began to bloom, the old Bearman sat on a stone every day until the sun set, and he was happy. "Eh, Bearman, they bloom every year; it never changes. Why don't we move on?" asked the bear. But the Bearman replied: "This time they are more beautiful than ever. They have never bloomed so beautifully."

That evening they made camp near a spring. After the story, they listened to the tiny melody. Then the Bearman took the horn and hung it around the bear's neck on a silver chain.

"It will bring you luck," he said. "It has to bring you luck!"

It was a warm night. The chorus of the frogs could be heard from all the pools, and the black beetles buzzed from stem to stem. But then it became so still that one could hear the rustling sound of falling stars. And as the bear slept, the man talked a long time to his friend, Dear God.

In the morning the bear shook the dewdrops off his fur, poked at the man with his nose and growled: "Get up, Bearman, the sun is shining!" The Bearman didn't move. The bear tugged at the man's legs and growled once more: "Bearman, the sun is shining, the sun is shining!" The Bearman didn't move.

The bear was surprised. Never in his whole life could he remember the Bearman sleeping so soundly. He scratched at the man's leg and growled: "The story, Bearman, the story!" The Bearman didn't answer. So the bear stood up on his hind legs and began to dance. He danced around the man in a circle, as he did at the fairs. "How's my dancing, Man? Good, eh?" he growled, and thought the man would now wink his eye and say: "Very good, Brown One, and so harmonious!" But the man was silent. "I'm leaving," the bear finally growled. He shuffled off, knowing that the man wouldn't let him travel alone. From time to time he stopped, listening for the scratching steps of the Bearman. After half a mile the bear turned and looked behind him. No one was there.

The bear trotted back. He sat down beside his friend and watched him as he slept. And he didn't budge from the Bearman's side, even though he was almost starving and his throat was parched from thirst. He laid his head on his front paws and growled sorrowfully.

On the third day, the postman came by. "Good morning, Bearman," he called. "Nice and warm today, eh?" As he came closer he saw that the Bearman was dead and the bear half-starved. The postman ran to the village and told the mayor and the farmers about it. And all the people came to the spring and saw that the Bearman was dead. The children brought food for the bear and the cabinet-maker made a coffin with seven silver buttons on the lid.

They buried the Bearman by the highway that was his home. And because they knew that he was a religious man, they cut the following epitaph on a stone:

> Here lies the Bearman. He traveled
> through the country, was a God-fearing man,
> could juggle seven balls,
> was a friend of children and all good people.
> God rest his soul. Amen.

And for a long time afterward the people talked about the unusual funeral procession—a procession in which a bear with a horn around his neck trotted behind the coffin, followed by so many children that there was hardly room for the grown-ups in the churchyard.

After the funeral they led the bear into the firehouse and locked and bolted the door. The elder farmers gathered at the mayor's house to discuss the bear's fate. The mayor spoke first: "Friends, the Bearman is dead—God rest his soul—and the bear is free for the asking. The bear is a good animal; he is strong and can be a great help to a farmer. So, whoever wants to take the bear, raise your right hand."

But there was nobody who wanted a bear, so no right hand was raised.

"What do we need a bear for?" cried the farmers. "Does he give milk like a cow?" they asked. "Can he pull a plow like an ox?" "No," they said, "a farmer has no use for a bear!"

The mayor said: "You could keep him on a chain like a dog to guard your house."

But the farmers replied: "He eats too much. A bear eats five times as much as a chained dog. You have to think of that!"

The next day the farmers traded the bear to eleven Gypsies who passed through the village. They got fifteen yards of wool cloth in return.

The bear was hitched to an iron chain and had to trot among starving dogs behind the Gypsy wagon. When he was too exhausted to take another step, the Gypsies would pull at his chain till his nose-ring cut into his flesh like red-hot iron, and they would lash him with their whips. He was also hungry and thirsty. The honey the children would bring him was gobbled up by the Gypsy women, and the bear didn't get a single drop. But the Bearman's horn still hung around his neck by the silver chain. He struck out furiously at anyone who tried to touch it.

The bear didn't die of hunger and pain because of Josho, who was his friend. Each night, as the Gypsies slept, Josho sneaked out to the bear. He cooled his wounds with herbs, he stole bread and honey for him, and he brought him water to drink. On cold nights the two huddled together under the wagon, and Josho warmed himself against the bear's fur and told him about the far-off lands through which the Gypsies had traveled.

One time he said: "You must remember that bears are not born to trot behind a wagon on a chain. Beyond the mountain, where the sun rises in the morning, is the land of deep forests. In the land of deep forests live wild bears. They hunt all day long. In the evening they go down to the streams to quench their thirst and at night they sleep in rock caves. In the spring they play together in the wide-open fields, and then the bear-children are born. The little bears are the size of small dogs, and as cheerful as the colorful birds."

The bear said: "I have never been in the land of deep forests."

Josho said: "All bears come from the land of deep forests. But sometimes men come into the deep forests and hide in the bushes close to a bear's cave. When the bear goes down to the stream in the evening, they enter the cave and steal the bear-children. They pierce the bears' noses with iron rings and put the bears on chains. Later, they keep jerking the chain upward till the pain is too much for the little bears, and they have to raise themselves up on their hind legs. This is how they learn to walk on two legs. After they have learned to walk on two legs, they are led onto a hot, iron platform. They have to keep hopping from one foot to the other, so as not to burn their soles. Music is played, and thus they learn to dance. Later on, whenever the bears hear music, they dance because they think that otherwise they will burn their soles. When they are big, they are sold to bearmen. By that time, they have forgotten the land of deep forests and believe that the only thing life can offer a bear is to be led on a chain and dance."

"I was never kept on a chain," said the bear. "The Bearman gave me honey, and every evening he told me a story about a star. I had a good life," he said. "But now I want to go to the land of deep forests."

Josho undid the chain and let the bear go free. "Farewell!" he said softly. "You must be careful; they will be looking for you. During the day you must hide yourself in the bushes."

Walking on velvet paws, the bear disappeared into the night. And in the sky he saw the black bear pulling the star-wagon and heard the call of the screech owl, and the air was fresh and tasted of leaves.

The way to the land of deep forests was long and dangerous. The bear had to swim across rivers and climb jagged mountains. During the rainy season, when the sun didn't come out, the bear often lost the way.

A couple of times he fell into a ravine and was almost suffocated in a snow-storm. Often he was close to starvation. And four times he was spotted by hunters and heard bullets whistle by.

When the colorful birds again returned from Africa, the bear reached the land of deep forests. He went up to the wild bears and said: "My name is Brown One and I'm a dancing bear. I have escaped from the Gypsies. Show me a cave where I can sleep." But before the wild bears could answer him, a very old she-bear spoke with venom: "Don't trust him! He has an iron ring through his nose. He works for humans, and he will spy on our caves. Don't trust him!"

Other wild bears also began to growl: "We don't trust you! You have an iron ring through your nose. You work for humans!"

"He must get the iron ring off and prove that he is a true bear, like us," nagged the old she-bear.

And other wild bears echoed: "Take off your iron ring to prove to us that you are a true bear, like us."

"I can't take it off," answered Brown One. "The humans, who stole me from my mother when I was very small, pierced my nose with the ring and welded the ends together."

"Anyone can say that," growled the wild bears. "You still have an iron ring through your nose and you work for humans. We don't want to have anything to do with you." They left him standing there and went on their way.

The bear was sad, for he believed that he would never succeed in taking the ring off.

He roamed through the woods like a free, wild bear. He didn't have to worry about hunger, and nobody came to put him on a chain. But he had no rock-cave which would shelter him from rain and storm, and he was despised by all wild bears.

And because he was always alone, his desire to see humans returned. And he would often stand at the edge of the forest and watch the farmers in the fields.

When summer came and the farmers cut the wheat, he saw how they sharpened their scythes with yellow rocks.

He looked for a yellow rock.

Day and night the bear rubbed his iron ring against the yellow rock,

and only seldom did he allow himself a short rest. On the twelfth day the iron was sawed through, and he could take the ring off.

Now, looking like a true bear, he went again to the wild bears. When they saw that he had taken off the ring, they welcomed him as one of their own and showed him a cave in which he could live. Nevertheless, the old she-bear muttered: "He still has a horn on a chain around his neck. A true bear doesn't have a horn on a chain around his neck!" But this time no one listened to her.

The dancing bear enjoyed the happy life with his shaggy companions. They hunted and nibbled berries and romped through the forest. And on Sundays they lay on their backs and let the sun warm them. They lay on their backs whenever they felt like it, even on working days.

Although the bear was happy and carefree, he could not forget the Bear-man. Often he dreamed about the village Fair and about the tiny melody. Sometimes he would go to the highway, look right and left, and then walk for miles through the white dust. And it seemed to him that he could hear the scratching footsteps of the Bearman.

In winter he had such a longing for humans that he dared to walk all the way to the edge of the village just to hear the ringing of bells and see the children.

On one such day, wolves had broken into a sheepfold and killed the sheep. All the men of the village went looking for the attackers, with dogs and torches.

Though the wind had blown away the wolves' tracks, when the men came to the edge of the forest, they saw the footprints of the bear.

They loaded their rifles with powder and lead, and lit new torches. In single file, they followed the footprints of the bear.

In the early hours of the morning they stood before his cave. The yelping of the dogs woke the bear, and then he heard the voices of the men.

Nothing aroused his rage more than the barking of dogs. Growling, the bear crouched down behind the entrance of his cave, and when the dogs rushed in he tore them apart with his paws.

"Murderer!" shouted the men. "Murderer! You have killed our sheep and now you have killed our dogs. You will pay for this!"

The bear raised himself on his hind legs and walked out of his cave. "Men," he growled, "I have not killed any sheep. I do not kill sheep. It is only your dogs I hate!"

At first the men couldn't believe their eyes when they saw a bear with a horn on a silver chain around his neck standing on his hind legs, and they made the sign of the cross. Then their rifles cracked. An agonizing pain tore through the bear's flanks.

He staggered. Blood gushed from his wounds. And while the men reloaded their firearms, the bear, with a great effort, crawled into the cave.

The men lit a fire in front of the cave and threw on wet leaves, and the wind carried a thick, biting smoke into the cave. "They want to smoke me out," thought the bear. "If I remain here I will suffocate."

Once again he gathered all his strength and crouched down to spring. With one single leap he landed on top of the smouldering leaves, beating them with his paws.

Smoke and flames scattered in all directions, and the men could not see each other in the thick smoke. They fired their rifles, but the bullets went astray. The bear plunged at the hunters, and everyone who could keep out of reach of his paws ran for his life.

When all the noise had died down, the bear dragged himself back into the cave. The pain throbbed in his loins, his flanks trembled, and his paws lay powerless on the ground. But he did not die. The storms on the highway and the whips of the Gypsies had made him strong. Gradually his wounds stopped bleeding and he fell into a long, deep sleep.

By the time the snow had melted in front of the bear's cave and the grass had begun to sprout, his wounds were healed and the old bear-strength returned to his body. He again roamed through the forest, admired by all the animals and feared by all the people.

For a long time after that, the bear avoided people. But he still longed for the highway; he still dreamed of the tiny melody; and he still loved the children and was happy when they came to the forest with their baskets and pots to gather berries.

On one of his wanderings the bear came across a small boy who was lost in the woods. Night was approaching and wolves were howling close by, so the bear took the boy into his cave.

The next morning the boy climbed on the shaggy shoulders of the bear and got a tight grip on the chain around the bear's neck. Then the bear and his rider trotted into the village. The boy shouted: "Giddyap, big dog, giddyap!" and the bear growled contentedly. And the people stood in front of their houses and made the sign of the cross and exclaimed: "How amazing!"

All day the bear lay in front of the boy's house like a faithful dog. Children came and brought him honey. And the bear growled with pleasure when they climbed on his shoulders and pulled his fur.

When the sun set he raised himself and went down the village street and out into the forest.

Proud and erect and taking only three steps to each breath.

Every evening from then on the bear would lie in front of his cave in the forest, his head resting on his front paws, and his ears pricked up. Beside him sat the boy. He would point to a star and tell the bear a story. Then the boy would take the horn from the bear's chain and play one single note. And the note was so beautiful that the trees stopped rustling and the forest seemed enchanted. And then the tiny melody followed. And it was as pure and clear as silver jewels. And people everywhere laid down their tools and listened to the sound from the forest.

Days passed and years passed. Winter came and the farmers and the young men gathered on the frozen lakes to play the game of curling, and the animals slept in their caves in the ground. There came the time of clear skies, and the apple trees and the whitethorn bushes were in bloom, and the colorful birds came from Africa. The yellow dust came, and the glitter over the highway, and the farmhands came out to cut the wheat. Indian summer brought a hundred thousand spiders who put a spell on the land, and the colorful birds again flew to Africa. And leaves died and bonfires burned. There came the time of cold mornings and frost and thin ice over puddles. And the storm came and the snow and a new winter.

The entertainers have long since stopped traveling along the highways, and there are no bears who can dance.

But the melody is still alive. The ragmen and the shepherds sometimes whistle it on their wooden flutes. And certain people traveling on the highways can hear it even today—in the humming of the telephone wires before a thunderstorm; or in the fall, when the wind sweeps through the leaves of trees.